BUFORD BEAR's
Bad News Blues

◆ ◆ ◆

H. Norman Wright
with **Gary J. Oliver**
Illustrated by Sharon Dahl

VICTOR BOOKS

A DIVISION OF SCRIPTURE PRESS PUBLICATIONS INC.
USA CANADA ENGLAND

A big, wet ball of water fell through the air. It landed in Buford Bear's bowler hat, along with the other tears which had dripped from his sad eyes.

Buford sat outside his den and sighed, "Oh me, oh my. I'm so sad. I wish I felt glad instead of so . . . bad!" Another tear fell with a splish and a splash.

Suddenly there was a bigger splash, and Buford was surprised to find a nut floating in his bowler. He looked up into the trees just in time to see Shirl Squirrel bouncing from limb to limb.

"Sorry about that!" said Shirl. "Am I bothering you?" She bounded down from one branch to the next, then jumped the last three feet to the ground. "What's wrong, Buford Bear?"

The grass behind Buford rustled, and a pair of pink ears belonging to Hip Hop Bunny were soon followed by the rabbit's worried face. "Yeah. I heard you sniffling and snuffling. Why the tears, big buddy?"

With a sniffle and a snuffle, and two more tears for good measure, Buford moaned, "Oh, woe is me. I'm just so sad. I wish I felt glad. But I feel so bad."

Shirl and Hip Hop looked at each other with surprise, then turned toward their friend.

"What's there to be sad about?" asked Shirl. "It's a pretty day. Look at all the grass and flowers to eat, the butterflies to chase, the hollow logs to crawl through."

"I don't care about those things," said Buford, with more sniffles than ever. "Anyway, the last time I tried to crawl through a hollow log, I got stuck."

Before Hip Hop could laugh at the idea of Buford stuck in a log, Buford shot him a mournful look. "And it's not funny, bunny. Nothing's funny anymore."

"**B**uford," Shirl said. "Let us help you. You've got a bad case of the blues and you need to talk to your friends. What's your problem, exactly?"

Buford said sadly, "Everything has gone wrong lately. And today doesn't look any brighter. No one understands. Maybe I'll feel this way forever and ever." Buford dumped out the tears from his soggy hat and plopped it back on his head.

"And don't even try to cheer me up," he added. "It won't help!"

"Don't you want to talk?" asked Hip Hop.

"I've been talking to somebody about my troubles," said the big bear.

"Who?" asked Shirl.

"Me, that's who," Buford replied.

"That's just the problem," said Hip Hop. "It's like one sad person talking to another sad person. It just makes you feel worse. Try talking to us now, okay?"

"Okay," said Buford with a very deep sigh. "It all started a few days ago when I was on my way to the pond. I passed Elwood Elk and Bruce Moose along the path, but they just ignored me. And Oscar and Oliver Otter just ran the other way when they saw me coming. I try to be friendly, but I think the other animals must not like me very much. Anyway, after that I decided to go on home to my den."

"Buford, we're your friends," said Shirl. "We think you're great! And the other woodland animals do too. They probably just didn't see you."

"Well, it doesn't feel that way to me right now."

"So what did you do next?" asked Hip Hop.

Buford sighed, remembering, "The next day it rained and rained, so I stayed inside my den all day long."

"Did you tell anyone else you were sad? Did you ask anyone to come over for a visit?" asked Shirl.

"No," said Buford.

"You mean you just moped around your dark, crowded, smelly den?"

"Maybe it's not the most cheerful place in the forest, but it is my home," said Buford with only a little hurt pride. "No, I didn't tell anyone my troubles. And I felt sadder and sadder to think that I was all alone. Then the really bad thing happened."

"What was that?" asked Hip Hop with concern.

Tears started to overflow from Buford's eyes again as he remembered. "The next day I felt a little better, so I decided to go across the woods to see my very best bear friend—Beulah Bear. When I got to her den, an old owl told me she had moved away, to the other side of the mountain. I don't think I'll ever see her again."

Hip Hop's face fell. "You know, my best bunny friend, Rad Rabbit, moved away last summer. I walked around with a sad face for the longest time. I didn't feel like doing much either."

"You mean it's normal to feel sad when you lose a friend?" asked Buford.

"Sure, it's normal," said Hip Hop, giving the bear a pat on his big brown paw.

"Oh my, Buford Bear," said Shirl, wringing out her tail which was now wet with the bear's big tears, "you do have a bad case of the blues. No wonder!"

"Just wait," said Buford. "It gets worse."

"After I found out about Beulah, I felt so low, I decided to visit my favorite berry patch. Nothing cheers me up like a mouthful of wild blueberries. So I hiked back across the woods to my secret spot. And it was gone! I guess the lightning from the storm a few days ago hit a nearby tree. The fire from the tree also burned up my berries!"

Buford sighed a deep sigh and rested his head in his hands. "This hasn't been my week," he said. "When I think about those lost berries, I get even sadder than before."

"Everyone is sad when they lose something that was important to them," said Shirl gently. "I lost my nest and half a tree full of nuts when lightning hit my last home. Sure, I was glad to get out safely, but I cried and cried about all my nice things and hard work—gone up in smoke. Losing things can be very hard. But it got better in time."

"So time can help? That's good to know," said Buford. "And talking with you has made me feel better. What else can I do?"

"I know," said Shirl, "let's all think about what we can do to help get rid of Buford's blues. You too, bear. Now that you've stopped crying, you can help make a plan."

The animals decided to think about their ideas in private.

Shirl whisked to the top of the tallest tree around and munched on a pine cone while she thought. "I've got it!" she said, finally.

Hip Hop burrowed into the grass, nibbling on some sweet clover nearby. "That's it!" he shouted after a while.

Buford stretched out in the warm sun, chewing on the honeycomb he'd saved for a special day. As he relaxed, he felt some of his sadness drain away. Suddenly, he sat straight up, saying, "Yes, yes, yes! Just the thing for my bad news blues!"

At the same time, the three animals met together by Buford's den.

"Listen to this," said Buford with excitement. "Why don't you two come hunting with me. Together we'll find a new berry patch, and share what we have with everybody."

"It'll be a party. A very bear-y blueberry party!" said Shirl, her tail twitching at the thought. "That's just what I was thinking of."

"Hey, you guys," said Hip Hop. "You stole my idea. It is a good one, isn't it? Blueberries to beat the blues."

"Say, why don't you ride up here with me?" invited Buford. So the three friends set off together.

Just then a butterfly landed itself squarely on Buford Bear's nose. His friends laughed out loud at the sight. And Buford suddenly found himself doing something he hadn't done for days.
He smiled.

Growing On:
How grownups can help a child cope with depression

Ask your child to give you his or her definition of depression. Ask: *Do you think sadness is good or bad? Where did you learn that?*

Explain that sadness is a God-given emotion which everyone experiences. There are different ways to express the sadness that all of us experience. Some ways are helpful and some do harm.

Talk about these questions:

★ Ask your child to talk to you about the times when he or she is sad.

☾ Share what made you sad when you were a child. What was your biggest loss as a child? Describe what you did that helped you over-come your sadness.

★ Read Psalm 88:1 and James 1:2 to your child. Encourage your child to talk to you about his or her losses.

☾ Explain to your child that sadness is normal. Ask: What can you do when you feel sad? Do you ever do some of the things Buford does? Which friends do you think helped Buford the most?

★ Talk together about things your child can do when sad or depressed. Encourage your child to (1) talk about it, (2) express his or her feelings about it, (3) look at both the loss and the positive things in life, and (4) if there was a loss, help your child say good-bye to whatever they lost. You may want to read chapters 4 and 6 in *Raising Emotionally Healthy Kids* (Victor Books) by these authors for additional help.

☾ Read the following passages with your child: "Lord, turn to me and be gracious to me, for I am lonely and afflicted. The troubles of my heart are multiplied; bring me out of my distresses" (Psalm 25:16, 17 AMP).

"For I know the plans I have for you," declares the Lord, "plans to prosper you, not to harm you, plans to give you hope and a future" (Jeremiah 29:11, NIV).

God is our refuge and strength, an ever-present help in trouble (Psalm 46:1, NIV).

*Grownups will find more information on this subject on pages 77–88 and 106–122 of *Raising Emotionally Healthy Kids* by H. Norman Wright and Gary J. Oliver, published by Victor Books.

Discover all the Wonder Woods books!
Ric and Rac's Woodland Adventure (Fear)
HipHop and His Famous Face (Anger)
Buford Bear's Bad News Blues (Sadness)
Bruce Moose and the What-Ifs (Worry)

Editor: Liz Duckworth
Designer: Andrea Boven
Production: Myrna Hasse

ISBN: 1-56476-461-3

1 2 3 4 5 6 7 8 9 10 Printing/Year 00 99 98 97 96